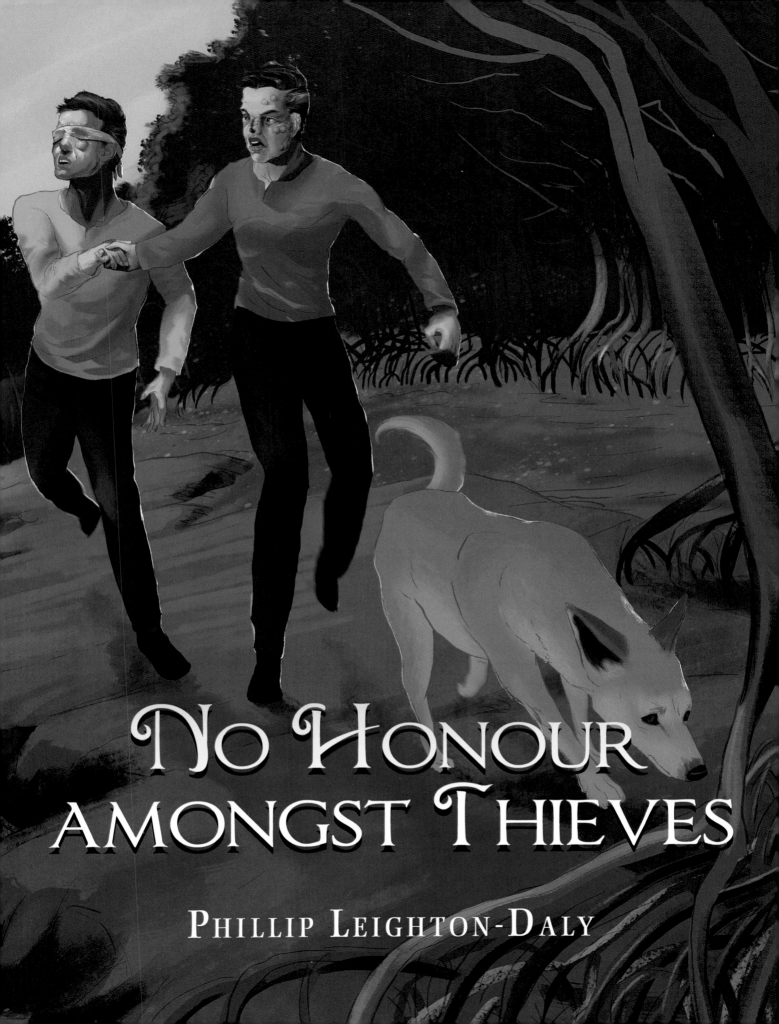

No Honour Amongst Thieves

Phillip Leighton-Daly

To order additional copies of this book, contact:
Xlibris
1-800-455-039
www.xlibris.com.au
Orders@Xlibris.com.au

Illustrated by Windel Eborlas

ISBN: Softcover   978-1-7960-0507-3
         Hardcover   978-1-7960-0508-0
         EBook   978-1-7960-0506-6

Print information available on the last page

Rev. date: 09/12/2019

No Honour Amongst Thieves

Phillip Leighton-Daly

Illustrated by Windel Eborlas

Several months after the old fisherman's death, twin brothers Joshua and Joseph moved into his ramshackle bungalow on the escarpment. Both had contracted leprosy in their youth and spent the last thirty years in the leper colony, where they had been

Sadly, they had witnessed the disease's distressing onset and its insidious progression. Leprosy had dealt them cruel hands. Joshua's ability to blink had been destroyed. Gone were the moisturizing and cleaning mechanisms of his eyes. Now infected and dried, they appeared as blackened sockets. Joseph had suffered differently, though in no lesser degree. The cartilage in his nose had been eaten away, and his nostrils had collapsed. Additionally, he had lost the cartilage in both ears and most of his toes.

The brothers fished off the rocky shelves, as had the old fisherman. The pair straggled down the mountain in a curious fashion. With rods slung over his shoulder, Joe led the way; Josh trailed to the side, holding tightly to his brother's hand. Their dog, a dingo called Rem, was a constant companion.

At the water's edge, they crossed the narrow land bridge. In fair weather, even when the tide was full and water lapped each end of the arched causeway, they made the crossing. But when fierce winds prevailed and thunderous waves pummelled the bridge, a great anxiety welled inside them. The brothers sensed horror and dread in the dark, swirling water beneath the land bridge. The old man had named this "the Maelstrom." During such times, they never risked a crossing, choosing instead to pass through a swamp of treacherous quicksand.

The brothers moved cautiously around the rock shelves. They anticipated cruel reprisals from the wicked mermaid queen. News of her ruthless antics had spread throughout the region.

For months after the old man's death, the mermaid queen seethed with resentment. She had failed to exhibit the old man's bones in her palace. The seagulls, those vicious imposters, were the queen's informants. It was from them that the queen had learned of the old man's demise.

The disfigurement of the brothers was a curiosity to the merfolk, who did not physically age and appeared immune to disease. For the merfolk, the opportunity to study what they called "carnival exhibits" was unique. Tours were organised to view what was touted as the "Encounter with Freaks." Excursions were widely advertised by the mermaid queen. A chariot conveyed a select community around the rock shelves. Such an entourage presented a macabre spectre. Imagine a chariot drawn by six tiger sharks, an escort of four bull rays, and a brutish merman at the helm.

To witness such a premier attraction demanded an exorbitant price. One gold bar from the wreck of a galleon named Epoch was the cost. Collection of this treasure was not without horrific risk. The Epoch lay in a deep trench. Treacherous currents scoured the ocean floor, creating effects similar to the aftermath of a great glacier.

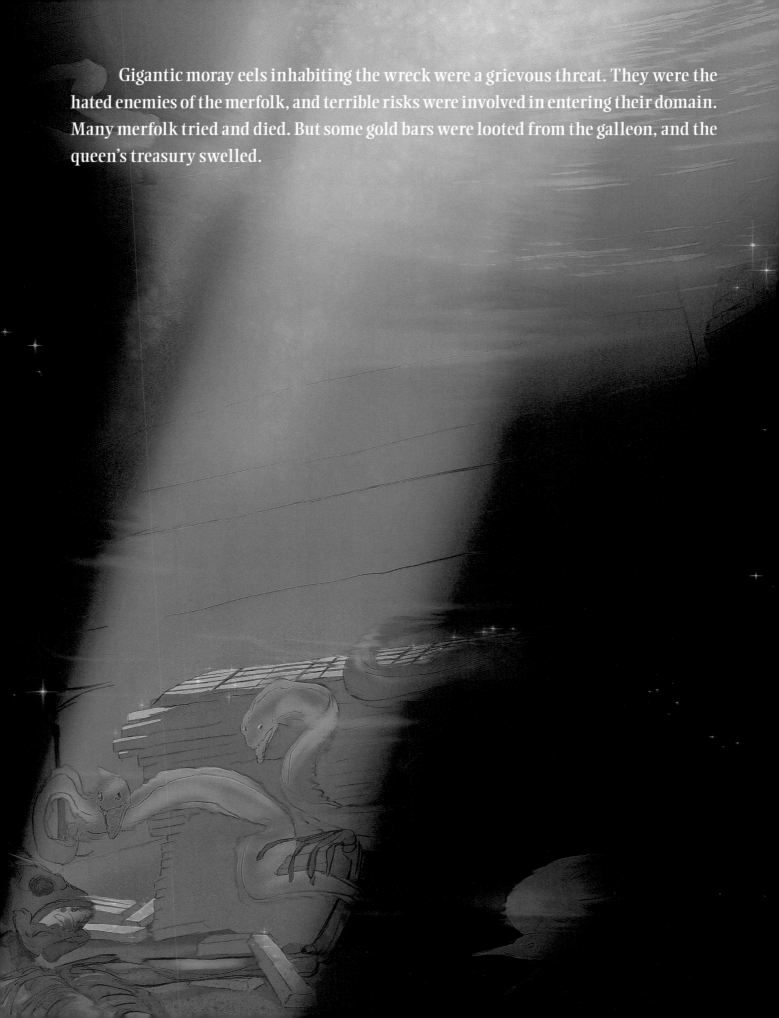

Gigantic moray eels inhabiting the wreck were a grievous threat. They were the hated enemies of the merfolk, and terrible risks were involved in entering their domain. Many merfolk tried and died. But some gold bars were looted from the galleon, and the queen's treasury swelled.

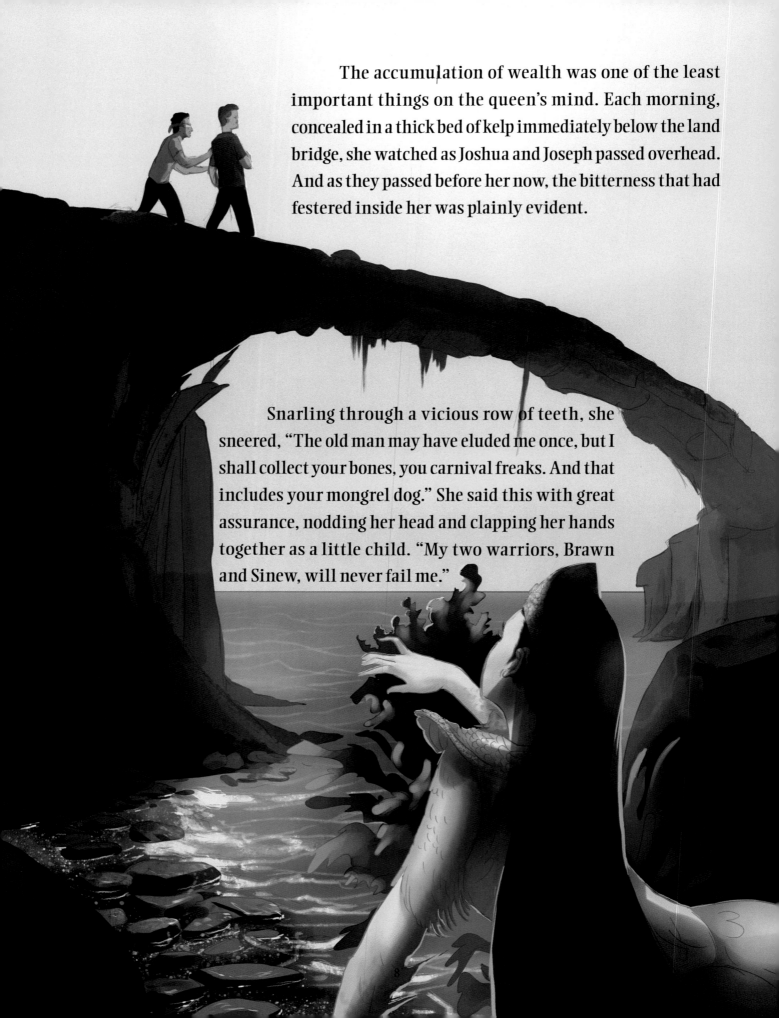

The accumulation of wealth was one of the least important things on the queen's mind. Each morning, concealed in a thick bed of kelp immediately below the land bridge, she watched as Joshua and Joseph passed overhead. And as they passed before her now, the bitterness that had festered inside her was plainly evident.

Snarling through a vicious row of teeth, she sneered, "The old man may have eluded me once, but I shall collect your bones, you carnival freaks. And that includes your mongrel dog." She said this with great assurance, nodding her head and clapping her hands together as a little child. "My two warriors, Brawn and Sinew, will never fail me."

Early one morning, Josh was the first to harken to the frenzied shrieks of the gulls as the brothers wound down the mountainside. His hearing had sharpened to compensate for his loss of sight. Joe noted his brother's warning, but it was not until they reached the land bridge that he stopped, mesmerized in frightful dread.

There, immediately in front of them, lay a large merman on the land bridge. He grinned threateningly. His upper body was supported in a semi-upright position on his large muscular arms.

Hearing peculiar sloshing behind him, Joe turned around. Another brute had slunk up from behind, swinging a net fashioned from seaweed. With the brothers' escape up the mountain blocked, Joe had little option but to lead Josh into the swamp. Rem followed closely.

The brothers were very much aware of the danger here. On a recent incursion, they had seen the quicksand swallow a young mountain goat. Painstaking care probing the ground was one means of safe passage. But there was little time for that; the mermen were closing in rapidly.

Curiously, there was another way through the quicksand—good old Rem. Sniffing the swamp intently, their loyal companion led them deeper and deeper into the wasteland. He weaved around irregularly, determining secure passage. Still, the brutish monsters appeared to be quickly gaining on them.

But to their peril, the mermen opted to scramble directly towards the brothers. With dreadful screams and a furious flailing of their arms, they sank quickly into the mire. Frothy bubbles on the muddy surface were the sole traces of any tragedy.

For several weeks, the mermaid queen lay beneath the Maelstrom, watching the brothers anxiously for clues of her warriors' whereabouts. Long after their departure, she flattened out pathetically on the rock shelf, tearing at the rock with her fingernails and crying mournfully for her champions, Sinew and Brawn.

Finally, learning from the gulls about their misfortune, she slunk as a skulking dog back to palace, living as a recluse and rarely venturing outside the confines of her kingdom.

Throughout the brothers' lives, trouble rarely travelled alone. Close by the Devil's Craw on the Great Plateau, a hoard of bushrangers lived in an obsolete mining town pockmarked with mining shafts. Despite their disabilities, the brothers deprived much pleasure scavenging through the collapsing shafts.

A wicked element of the bushranger hoard deeply resented intruders encroaching into their domain. The bodies of those caught in the mines were unceremoniously thrown upon the Putrid Pit, where wild pigs and crows feasted upon their flesh. This macabre scene served as an intimidatory warning for those contemplating passage there.

Though the brothers had been warned often enough of these dangers, they chose to take little heed, for their entire lives were coloured by misfortune and hardship. Unfortunately, the brothers' lives became terrifyingly intertwined with those of the murderous bushranging element, Curley Bill and Stretch McGaw. In a large shaft, these notorious bushrangers, with revolvers drawn, startled Josh and Joe.

"Now look who we have here, Don Juan and Blind Freddy," quipped Curley Bill, referring to Joseph's disfigured face and to Joshua's blackened eye sockets. Strange they would say this as the outlaws themselves were filthy, uncouth vagabonds. Their unsightly teeth were blackened and diseased, their hair dishevelled and flailing.

"Meddlers aren't welcome here, carnival freaks," added Stretch. His vile breath reeked of alcohol. "All visitors will be graciously welcomed at the Putrid Pit. We'll steal away your lives, and our crows will assuredly pick all the flesh from your bones!" Their booming laughter echoed through the mine.

But at the very moment when they least expected it, Rem lurched at Curley Bill. He tumbled awkwardly into the rotted pit prop, which collapsed under his weight. A curtain of dust blanketed the shaft as Stretch fired off several shots. Rem, isolated from his masters, scampered from the mine, narrowly evading Stretch McGaw's wild and wayward gunfire.

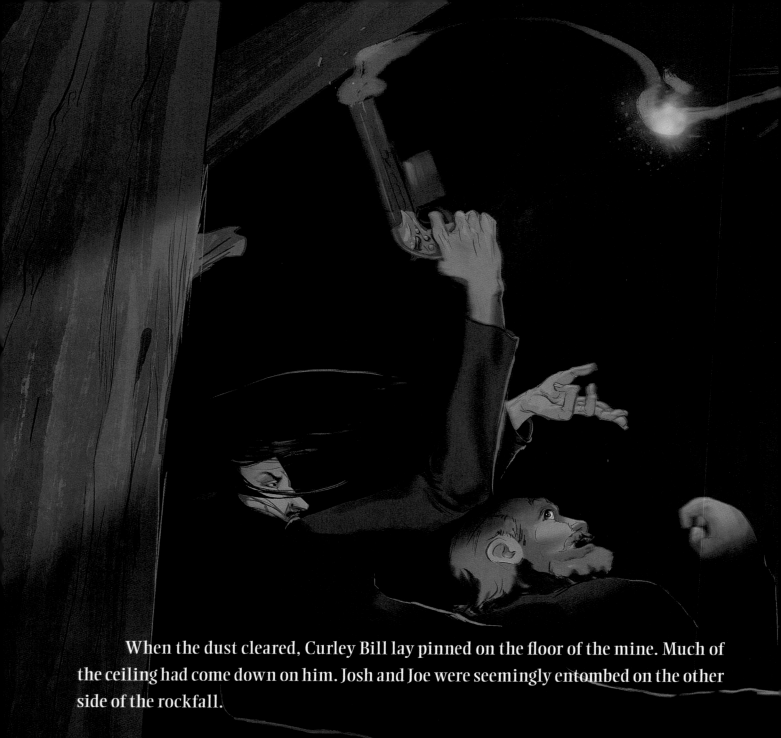

When the dust cleared, Curley Bill lay pinned on the floor of the mine. Much of the ceiling had come down on him. Josh and Joe were seemingly entombed on the other side of the rockfall.

The brothers were forced further and further into the blackness, distancing themselves from the swirling dust. Strangely, their roles were reversed. Josh grasped his brother's hand and moved more assuredly through the blackness than Joe. Faint recollections from a previous visit indicated that the passage forked ahead. Feeling their way along the rockface, they noted that one passage descended deep into the mountain, while the right passage rose steeply. Along the latter they proceeded, their spirits rising as a fresh current of air descended upon them. A distant light illuminated the path further ahead. Oddly, too, they walked on tram tracks.

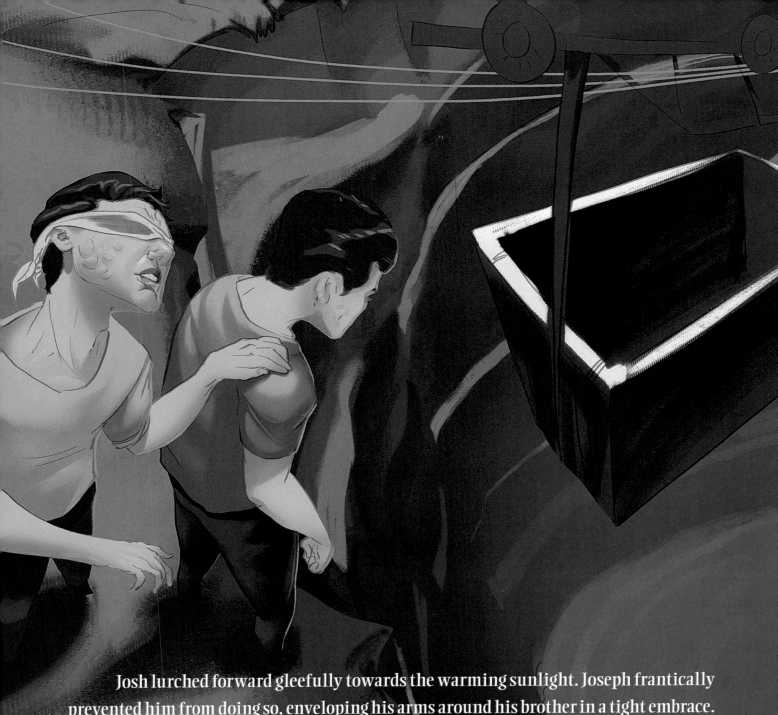

Josh lurched forward gleefully towards the warming sunlight. Joseph frantically prevented him from doing so, enveloping his arms around his brother in a tight embrace. "Don't you dare move a muscle, Josh!"

If he had, it would indeed have been his last step. Joshua stood perched on the brink of a cliff high on the mountain. Such was the sheerness of that terrain that no vegetation had established a foothold there.

Looking down, Joe perceived tiny figures hustling into the mine. He later watched as the group emerged from the mountainside, carrying who he thought was the injured Curley Bill.

For an indeterminable period, Josh said nothing, his mind both shocked and awash with thoughts of plunging to his death over a glaring abyss. When he did recover, he asked, "Where's Rem?"

"I have no idea," Joe replied.

"What now then?" inquired Josh. "We can't climb down? There's the passage we passed on our left. Maybe we can dig ourselves out where the tunnel collapsed."

"There is another way," Joe replied. "Ore from inside the mine was once loaded into trolleys and pushed up to where you are standing." The tram lines lay beneath their feet. "A flying fox descended to a collection and processing plant below." Joe gestured down the mountainside. Then, realizing the futility of gesturing to a blind man, he continued, "There's a basket to our left. We'll climb aboard and glide down to the works. The derelict plant lies close by the mining town. Keep deadly silent, Josh. We don't want a hoard of bushrangers on our heels."

At dusk, Joe assisted his brother into the iron cradle. Clambering aboard himself, he pushed out into the great void. This involved considerable risk, of course, but the brothers seemed oblivious of that. If the iron cable broke, its human passengers would plummet hundreds of feet to their deaths. Or say the cable car stalled midway down. The brothers would be trapped indefinitely hundreds of feet above the ground!

But the cables held securely. And virtually without a sound, the cable car berthed at the bottom of the mountain. And guess who strode up excitedly to welcome them? Rem! "Just as well dingoes don't bark," quipped Joe in a hushed tone.

"I've rarely ever heard him howl," added his brother.

Safely home, the brothers slept fitfully, recalling their perilous adventure. Rem was reunited with them, and from that, they drew much comfort and calm.

Earlier that day, Curley was stretchered reluctantly back to the mining town by the bushrangers. I say "reluctantly" for he never had one kind word to say to anyone. And as he rarely washed, he reeked horribly. Because of his unsanitary ways, his injured leg grew gangrenous. In the absence of surgeons, the amputation resembled a mutilation. With an absence of craftsmen, a wooden appendage was hastily fashioned out of the curved leg of a crude armchair.

My, how the tide had turned in Curley's world. Whereas once he had cruelly mocked and mimicked the brothers, the bushrangers were now returning the same. Wisecracks directed to him such as, "May I have the next dance, pet?" did little to sweeten his sour disposition.

Curley's and Stretch's unsavoury ways, their drunkenness, and their absolute disrespect for life saw them despised by the other bushrangers. Certainly, there was no honour between them and the other bushrangers.

Curley blamed the brothers for the loss of his leg. When news of their escape from the mine was passed on to him, a horrible anger welled up inside. Along with the impressionable Stretch McGaw, they schemed to exact the cruellest imaginable revenge on Joe and Josh.

The other bushrangers knew nothing of Curley's or Stretch's cruel intentions. They clearly believed that Curley had brought this misfortune upon himself. Their grievances were with the corrupt authorities. The bushrangers supported both the mission and leper colony. Never once had they impeded the old fisherman's sojourns through their territory. Sentries stationed along the mountains had ensured that the old man arrived safely at the leper colony and the mission.

The brothers were occasionally visited by an old friend, Tom, the boundary rider. Tom patrolled the immense pastoral boundaries on the Great Plateau and beyond, into the western desert. He repaired fences, killed feral pests, and tended to injured animals. Tom had a sincere concern for the brothers. He had advised them against moving out of the leper colony, away from the care and support it provided. Of late, Tom visited more frequently because he felt that their health was noticeably slipping.

The altercation with Curley and Stretch had a wearing effect on the brothers, and personnel from the mission and the colony often visited them to inquire of their welfare. Rarely did the brothers fish. And rarely did they venture onto the Great Plateau.

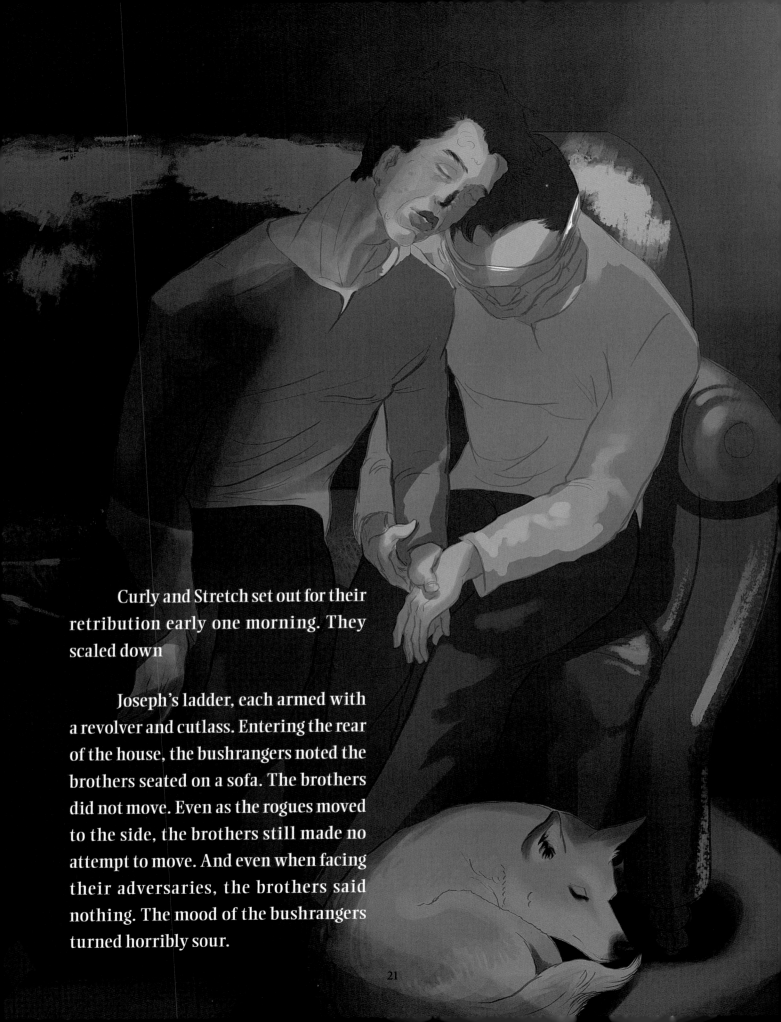

Curly and Stretch set out for their retribution early one morning. They scaled down

Joseph's ladder, each armed with a revolver and cutlass. Entering the rear of the house, the bushrangers noted the brothers seated on a sofa. The brothers did not move. Even as the rogues moved to the side, the brothers still made no attempt to move. And even when facing their adversaries, the brothers said nothing. The mood of the bushrangers turned horribly sour.

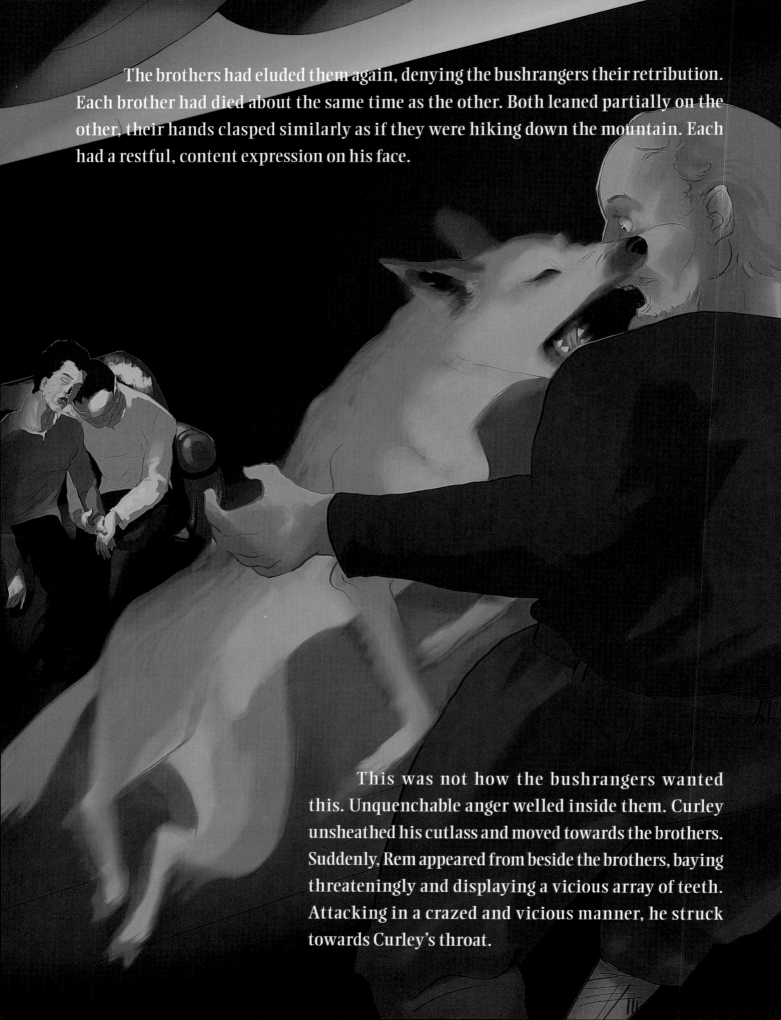

The brothers had eluded them again, denying the bushrangers their retribution. Each brother had died about the same time as the other. Both leaned partially on the other, their hands clasped similarly as if they were hiking down the mountain. Each had a restful, content expression on his face.

This was not how the bushrangers wanted this. Unquenchable anger welled inside them. Curley unsheathed his cutlass and moved towards the brothers. Suddenly, Rem appeared from beside the brothers, baying threateningly and displaying a vicious array of teeth. Attacking in a crazed and vicious manner, he struck towards Curley's throat.

Curley dealt him a deathly blow with his cutlass. And as he lay dying across the legs of his masters, the outlaws riddled his body with bullets. Then, cursing and reloading their revolvers, they fired indiscriminately inside the house. As cowardly curs, partially content with their handiwork, they slunk away.

They climbed up onto the Great Plateau and rode slowly back to the mining town, firing off shots and heavily drinking whisky.

24

As they passed the paddocks where Tom, the boundary rider, penned his camels, they wantonly shot the old bull called Harold, who had served Tom loyally in the western desert. Tom's younger camel narrowly escaped, a bullet striking a tree close behind where he had sheltered.

But they were not finished with old Harold. They roped and dragged him off to the Putrid Pit, a boastful sign of their mindless barbarity.

om was the first to encounter the distressing scene in the house. He also noted with great sadness the corpse of his old bull camel strewn across the Putrid Pit.

The bodies of the brothers and their dog were transported back to the leper colony. A service was attended by many. Tom was there, as was a contingent of bushrangers. Curley Bill and Stretch McGaw did not attend. At the service, mention was made of the brothers and their unwavering faithfulness through difficult times. Such concern was surely one of the highest human qualities. It was, according to the old padre, a special bond rarely evident between siblings.

Mention was also made of Rem and his unqualified loyalty irrespective of physical disfigurements. Harold and his unyielding service to Tom in the western desert was also honoured. General conversations regarding the wanton barbarism upon these loyal and hardworking animals were raised, and the bushrangers appeared noticeably affected by it. Withdrawing into a group, they muttered incessantly amongst themselves. Even prior to the end of the service, two bushrangers galloped off in the direction of the mining town at a furious pace.

After the funeral, on his return through the Devil's Craw, Tom was greatly heartened when he noted that old Harold had been buried. The camel's grave was marked with a wooden cross and bore the notation, "Harold, loyal and hardworking, never shirked one duty."

Further along the Devil's Craw, two corpses hung by the neck from the branch of a large gum. Both were horribly burnt. A calico sheet draped across them read, "Mindless killers of man and beast."

As ominous effigies, those bodies hung on their makeshift gibbet for five years. Of all the guff and menacing threats that had spewed from Curley's mouth, one certainly came to true. The crows did indeed pick all the flesh from his bones!

Printed in the United States
By Bookmasters